I LOVE TO SLEEP IN MY OWN BED

Written by Shelley Admont

Illustrated by Sonal Goyal, Sumit Sakhuja

First edition, 2014

Library and Archives Canada Cataloguing in Publication data

I love to sleep in my own bed/ Shelley Admont

ISBN: 978-0-993700002 paperback
ISBN: 978-0-993700064 hardcover
ISBN: 978-1-926432014 ebook

Although the author and the publisher have made every effort to ensure the accuracy and completeness of information contained in this book, we assume no responsibility for errors , inaccuracies, omission or any inconsistency herein.

for those I love
the most

Jimmy, a little bunny, lived with his family in the forest. He lived in a beautiful house with his mom, dad, and two older brothers.

Jimmy didn't like to sleep in his own bed. One night, he brushed his teeth and before going to bed, he asked his mom, "Mom, can I sleep in your bed with you? I really don't like sleeping in my bed alone."

"Sweetie," said Mom, "everyone has his own bed, and your bed suits you just right."

"But, Mom, I don't like my bed at all," answered Jimmy. "I want to sleep in your bed."

"Let's do this," said Mom, "you get into your bed, and I'll hug you, tuck you in, and read you and your brothers a story. Then, I'll give you a kiss and sit with you until you fall asleep."

"Okay," agreed Jimmy, and he gave his mom a kiss.

Mom hugged Jimmy and read a bedtime story to her three children. During the story, the children fell asleep. Mom gave all of them a goodnight kiss and went to sleep in her bed in her room.

In the middle of the night, Jimmy woke up. He sat up in bed, looked around, and saw that Mom wasn't next to him. Then, he got out of bed, took his pillow and blanket, and sneaked quietly into Mom and Dad's room. Jimmy got into their bed, hugged Mom, and fell asleep. They slept like that the whole night until the morning.

The next night, Jimmy woke up again. He took his pillow and blanket, and tried to leave the room like the night before. But just then, his middle brother woke up.

"Jimmy, where are you going?" he asked.

"Ah, ahh...," Jimmy stuttered, "nowhere. Go back to sleep." He quickly ran to his mom and dad's room. Jimmy sneaked into their bed and pretended to sleep.

But his middle brother was wide awake. *I wonder what's happening here*, thought his brother and decided to follow Jimmy. When he discovered that Jimmy was sleeping in their mom and dad's bed, he was very upset. *So that's the way it is, is it?* he thought. *If Jimmy is allowed, then I want to also.*

With that, he got
into their parents'
bed as well!

Mom heard the strange noises, opened her eyes, and saw the two children in bed. She made room for them in the bed, by making do with a small corner of the bed for herself. Again, they slept like that the whole night until the morning.

On the third night, the same thing happened. Jimmy woke up, took his pillow and blanket, and went to his parents' room. His brother followed him again and got into their parents' bed together with his pillow and blanket.But this time, the oldest brother also woke up. *Something's not right here,* he thought and followed his two younger brothers to Mom and Dad's room.

When the oldest brother saw his two brothers sleeping together with Mom and Dad, he was very jealous. *I also want to sleep in Mom and Dad's bed,* he thought and quietly jumped into the bed.

They slept like this the whole night. It was really uncomfortable. Mom and Dad didn't rest the whole night. Tossing and turning, they tried to find the most comfortable way to sleep. It wasn't easy for the little bunnies either. They turned over and over in the bed until it was almost morning.

Then suddenly...Boom! ...Bang! ...the bed broke!

"What happened?" Jimmy shouted as he woke up right away.

"Humph!" screamed the middle brother, who also woke up.

"Ooff!" yelled the oldest brother while lying on the floor.

"What are we going to do now?"
said Mom sadly.

"We'll have to build a new bed," Dad announced. "After breakfast, we'll go to the forest and start working."

After breakfast, the whole family went to the forest to build a new bed. After a whole day's work, they had made a big, strong bed out of wood. The only thing left to do was decorate it.

"We've decided to paint our bed brown," said Mom, "and while we're painting our bed, you can repaint your beds whatever colors you like."

"I want blue," said the oldest brother with excitement and ran to paint his bed blue.

"And I choose the color green," said the middle brother happily.

Jimmy took the color red and the color yellow. He mixed the red with the yellow and made his favorite color...orange! He painted his bed orange and decorated it with red and yellow stars. There were big stars and middle-size stars and even very, very small stars. After he finished, he ran to Mom and proudly shouted, "Mom, look at my beautiful bed! I love my bed so much. I want to sleep in it every night."

Mom smiled and gave Jimmy a big hug. Ever since then, Jimmy has slept in his orange bed every night.

Goodnight, Jimmy!

MORE GREAT BOOKS BY SHELLEY ADMONT

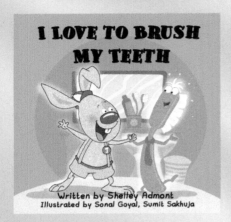

I LOVE TO BRUSH MY TEETH

Written by Shelley Admont
Illustrated by Sonal Goyal, Sumit Sakhuja

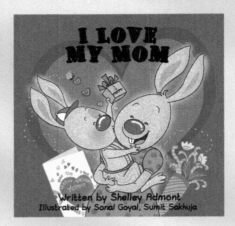

I LOVE MY MOM

Written by Shelley Admont
Illustrated by Sonal Goyal, Sumit Sakhuja

I LOVE TO GO TO DAYCARE

Written by Shelley Admont
Illustrated by Sonal Goyal, Sumit Sakhuja

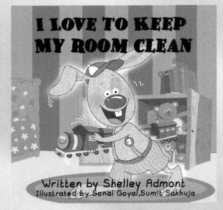

I LOVE TO KEEP MY ROOM CLEAN

Written by Shelley Admont
Illustrated by Sonal Goyal, Sumit Sakhuja

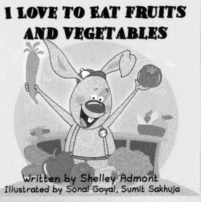

I LOVE TO EAT FRUITS AND VEGETABLES

Written by Shelley Admont
Illustrated by Sonal Goyal, Sumit Sakhuja

Written by
Shelley Admont

AMANDA'S DREAM

Illustrated by
Sumana Roy

Written by
Shelley Admont

AMANDA and the LOST TIME

Illustrated by
Humpty Dumpty

MOMMY

CPSIA information can be obtained at www.ICGtesting.com
Printed in the USA
LVOW05*1912220415

435650LV00011B/22/P